W9-DDO-194

Tell, Cathy Ann
The Classic tale of Mr.
Jeremy Fisher

9.95

DATE DUE			
JUL 0 6 1993 6/28			
AUG 0 9 1993 7/19			
SEP 0 7 1993			
SEP 2 1 1993			
SEP 2 8 1993			
OCT 2 0 1993			
NOV 1 6 1993			
DEC -9 1993			
DEC 2 7 1993			
JAN 1 8 1994			
APR 0 4 1994			

/2
LA
4/07
H6

MEDIALOG INC
ALEXANDRIA KY 41001

JUN 10 '93

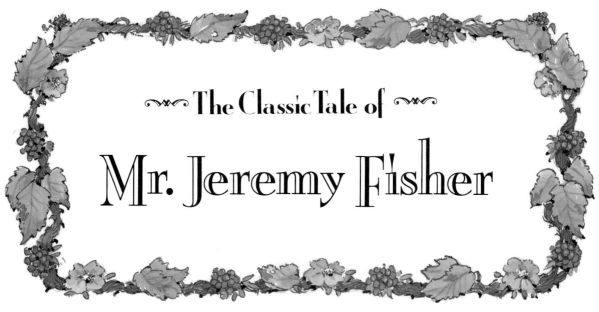

~ The Classic Tale of ~
Mr. Jeremy Fisher

Louis Weber, C.E.O.
Publications International, Ltd.
7373 North Cicero Avenue
Lincolnwood, Illinois 60646

JUN 1 0 '93

Permission is never granted for commercial purposes.

Based on the original story by Beatrix Potter
with all new illustrations

Manufactured in U.S.A.

8   7   6   5   4   3   2   1

ISBN 1-56173-596-5

Cover illustration by Anita Nelson

Book illustrations by Sam Thiewes

Adapted by: Cathy Ann Tell

HTS ❦ BOOKS
AN IMPRINT OF FOREST HOUSE™
School & Library Edition

Once upon a time there was a frog named Mr. Jeremy Fisher. He lived in a little damp house among the buttercups at the edge of a pond. The water was all slippy sloppy in his kitchen and by his back door. But Mr. Jeremy liked getting his feet wet. Nobody ever scolded him, and he never caught a cold!

He was quite pleased one day when he looked out and saw large drops of rain splashing in the pond.

"I will get some worms and go fishing and catch a dish of minnows for my dinner," said Mr. Jeremy Fisher. "If I catch more than five fish, I will invite my friends, Mr. Alderman Ptolemy Tortoise and Sir Isaac Newton, to dine with me. Mr. Tortoise, however, eats only salad."

Mr. Jeremy put on a raincoat and a pair of rubber overshoes. He took his fishing rod and basket and set off with enormous hops to the place where he kept his boat.

The boat was round and green and very much like the other lily pads. It was tied to a water plant in the middle of the pond.

Using a twig pole, Mr. Jeremy pushed the lily-pad boat out into open water. "I know a good place for minnows," he said.

Mr. Jeremy stuck his pole into the muddy bottom of the pond and fastened his boat to it. Then he settled himself cross-legged and arranged his fishing tackle. He had the dearest little red bobber. His rod was a tough stalk of grass. His fishing line was a long strand of horsehair. He hooked a little wiggly worm at the end of the line.

The rain trickled down his back, and for nearly an hour he stared at the bobber. "This is getting tiresome," said Mr. Jeremy Fisher. "I think I would like some lunch."

He pushed his boat back among the water grasses at the edge of the pond. Then he took some lunch out of his basket. "I will eat a butterfly sandwich and wait until the shower is over," said Mr. Jeremy Fisher.

Just then a water beetle swam under the lily-pad boat and tweaked Mr. Jeremy's toe! Mr. Jeremy crossed his legs up and out of reach, and went on eating his butterfly sandwich.

Once or twice something moved about the pond's edge with a rustle and a splash. "I certainly hope that is not a rat," said Mr. Jeremy Fisher. "I think I had better get away from here."

Mr. Jeremy shoved the boat a little way from shore and dropped in his fishing line. There was a bite almost immediately! The bobber went way under the water! "A minnow! A minnow! I have him by the nose!" cried Mr. Jeremy Fisher, pulling up on his rod.

But what a horrible surprise! Instead of a smooth fat minnow, Mr. Jeremy had caught a huge fish covered with sharp spines! The big fish snapped and flopped about, sticking Mr. Jeremy, until it was quite out of breath.

After the big spiny fish finished flopping around, it jumped back into the water.

A school of minnows put their heads out of the water and laughed at Mr. Jeremy Fisher.

Mr. Jeremy sat sadly on the edge of the lily pad, sucking his sore fingers and peering into the water. Suddenly, a *much* worse thing happened. It would have been a really *frightful* thing if Mr. Jeremy had not been wearing his raincoat!

An enormous trout jumped—*ker flop-p-p-p!*—with a splash. It seized Mr. Jeremy with a snap!

"Ow! Ow! Ow!" cried Mr. Jeremy. The trout turned and dove to the bottom of the pond!

But the trout didn't like the taste of the raincoat. In less than half a minute it spit Mr. Jeremy out! The only things it swallowed were Mr. Jeremy's rubber overshoes.

Mr. Jeremy bobbed up to the surface of the water like a cork. He swam with all his might to the edge of the pond. He scrambled out of the water and hopped home across the meadow with his raincoat all in tatters.

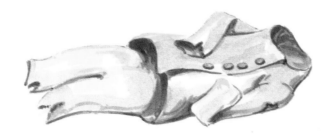

"What a mercy that was not an even bigger fish!" said Mr. Jeremy. "I have lost my rod and basket, but it does not much matter. I am sure I will never dare to go fishing again!"

That evening he bandaged his fingers and invited his friends to dinner. He could not offer them fish, but he had something else in the pantry.

His guests soon arrived. Sir Isaac Newton wore his black and gold waistcoat. Mr. Alderman Ptolemy Tortoise brought a salad with him in a string bag.

Instead of a nice dish of minnows, Mr. Jeremy served
Mr. Tortoise and Sir Isaac Newton a roasted
grasshopper with ladybug sauce for dinner. Frogs
consider it a beautiful treat, but *I* think it would
have been awful!